AN EDWARD THE UNREADY BOOK

EDWARD
IN DEEP WATER

· ROSEMARY WELLS ·

Dial Books for Young Readers *New York*

for Mimi

"Edward," asked Edward's mother,
"are you ready for Georgina's birthday party?"

"The party's at the town swimming pool," Edward's father said. "Let's get your swimsuit out!"

"We'll wrap Georgina's present in the prettiest paper,"
said Edward's mother.

"How about leaving your water wings home this time?"
his mother suggested.

"You swam last summer without water wings,"
Edward's father reminded Edward.

But Edward would not take off his water wings.

Georgina's mother welcomed Edward to the party.

Everybody sang "Happy Birthday, Georgina!"

Edward was the only one wearing water wings.

He heard Georgina whisper to her best friend, Ivy,
"Only sissies wear water wings!"

But Edward would not take them off.

"He's so sweet, let's give him a great big hug!"
whispered Georgina to Ivy.

Georgina and Ivy hugged Edward so tight,
they popped his water wings.

"Oops!" they said.

Within seconds the lifeguard rescued Edward.

Everyone was so worried that they sang
"Happy Birthday to Edward!" three times.

The lifeguard called Edward's mother and father.

"He's just not ready for this kind of party,"
said the lifeguard.

"Not everyone is ready for the same things at the same time," said Edward's mother and father.

On the way home Edward asked for
new water wings.

Just in case.

Published by Dial Books for Young Readers
A Division of Penguin Books USA Inc.
375 Hudson Street
New York, New York 10014

Library of Congress Cataloging in Publication Data
Wells, Rosemary.
Edward in deep water / Rosemary Wells.
p.   cm.—(Edward the unready)
Summary: Edward, a shy young bear, is not ready
for birthday pool parties with high-spirited bears.
ISBN 0-8037-1882-9
[1. Bears—Fiction. 2. Fear—Fiction.
3. Birthdays—Fiction. 4. Swimming—Fiction.]
I. Title. II. Series: Wells, Rosemary. Edward the unready.
PZ7.W46843Ec 1995 [E]—dc20 95-7884 CIP AC

*The artwork for each picture
is an ink drawing with watercolor painting.*

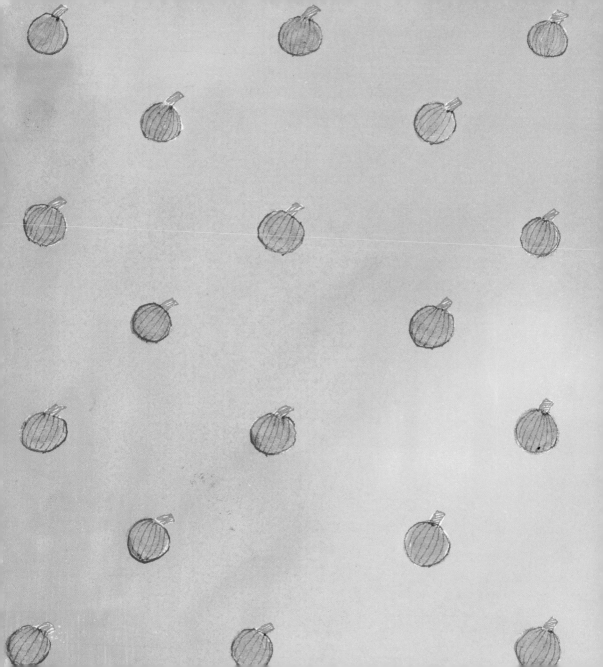